This book belongs to

....

Tips for the Storyteller

You're a Big Bear Now, Winston Brown is a humorous story about a little bear who wants to be grown up. All children who long to be big will identify with Winston's frustrations.

Keep reading to find out how to get the most fun out of this story.

Share the storytelling

Encourage your child to take an active part in the storytelling. Point to the words as you read them, let her turn the pages, and stop and talk about the pictures together. Encourage your child to shout out the repeated phrase, "I'm not little!" every time Winston is called "little" in the story. Knowing parts of the story will increase her confidence in reading.

Enjoy the excitement

Bring out the drama by reading with expression and doing some of the actions. Snore like the "Somebody," thump your chest to make the sound of Winston's thumping heart, squeeze your eyes shut, puff out your chest, and growl to frighten the "Somebody" away. Encourage your child to do these actions, too. Try following the footprints in the pictures with your fingers to map out the burglar's progress.

Who is the "Somebody"?

If your child knows the story of Goldilocks and the three bears, she will be able to guess who the "Somebody" is. To help her, after you have shared the story, look back at the pictures and talk about what has taken place. Point out the three bowls of porridge, the three chairs, and the three beds. Describe the "Somebody," and if your child doesn't know it, read or tell the story of Goldilocks.

Who's big and strong?

Ask your child why she thinks Winston doesn't want to be little. Does she want to be big and grown up? Or does she think that it's nice to be little and looked after? Ask her what's good about being little and what's good about being grown up. You could also talk about how it feels to be short or tall. What things can you do if you're little, and what things can you do if you're tall?

Enjoy the humor and excitement of the story!

For Oliver and Thea – Paul May

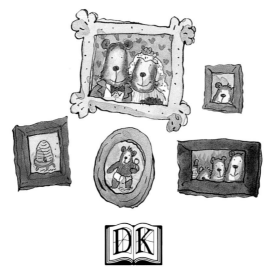

DK

LONDON, NEW YORK, SYDNEY, DELHI, PARIS,
MUNICH, and JOHANNESBURG

First American Edition, 2001
Published in the United States by
DK Publishing, Inc.
95 Madison Avenue
New York, New York 10016

01 02 03 04 05 10 9 8 7 6 5 4 3 2 1

Library of Congress Cataloging-in-Publication Data
May, Paul, 1953 -
You're a big bear now, Winston Brown! / by Paul May ; illustrated by Selina Young. - 1st American ed.
p. cm. - (Share-a-story)
Summary: His parents keep forgetting that Winston is a big bear now, but when he discovers a burglar in the house
who has eaten all of his porridge, Winston proves that he is both big and brave.
ISBN 0-7894-7896-X - ISBN 0-7894-7897-8 (pbk.)
[I. Growth - Fiction. 2. Courage - Fiction. 3. Bears - Fiction 4. Characters in literature - Fiction]
I. Young, Selina ill. II. Title. III. Share-a-story (DK Publishing, Inc.)
PZ7. M4545 Yo 2001   [E] - dc21   2001028506
Color reproduction by Dot Gradations, UK. Printed in Hong Kong by Wing King Tong
Acknowledgments: Series Reading Consultant: Wendy Cooling   **Activities Advisor:** Dawn Sirett
Photographer: Zara Ronchi   **Models:** Poppy Power, Kaya Thompson, and Mark Thompson

see our complete
catalog at
www.dk.com

You're a big bear now, Winston Brown

by Paul May

illustrated by
Selina Young

DK Publishing, Inc.

Winston Brown was having porridge for breakfast – again.

"Eat up, little bear," said Mr. Brown,
"or you won't grow up big and strong like me."
"I'm not little!" said Winston, but he picked up
his spoon and began to eat.

"Ouch!" he yelled. "This is too hot!"

"Poor Winston," said Mrs. Brown.

"Let's go for a walk in the woods while
we wait for our porridge to cool.
Come along, little bear."

"I'm *not* little," grumbled Winston Brown.

Outside, the sun was shining, but Winston was in a bad mood. His mouth hurt, and he was hungry.

"Why don't you two race to that tree?" said Mrs. Brown. "Great idea!" said Mr. Brown. "I was a champion runner once, you know."

Winston drew a starting line with a stick.
"Ready, set . . ."

"GO!" yelled Mrs. Brown.
Winston took off down the path.

Mr. Brown sprinted after him,
but Winston won by a whisker.
"You're too fast for me,"
gasped Mr. Brown.
Winston beamed.

"You're the fastest bear in
the family!" said Mrs. Brown,
patting him on the head.

Winston ran down the path and hid behind a bush. "ROAR!" he cried, as he sprang out at Mr. Brown.

They rolled over and over, growling at each other. "I used to be a champion wrestler," panted Mr. Brown. He pinned Winston to the ground.

"Ahem!" coughed Mrs. Brown.
Mr. Brown looked up and Winston saw his chance. He heaved – and there was Mr. Brown, flat on his back!

"Enough!" grunted Mr. Brown.
"You're too strong for me."
Winston grinned. Now he was definitely hungry.

"Do you think my porridge will be cool?" he asked.

"I expect so, little bear," said Mrs. Brown.

"Run on ahead and see."

"I'm not little!" yelled Winston,
as he ran through the trees.

He dashed up the walk

and skidded in through
the open door.

Winston stopped and stared. There were
big, muddy footprints on the floor.
"There's been a burglar," said Winston.
"Here, in our house!"

Winston's tummy rumbled. "I'll just try some
porridge," he thought, "and then I'll investigate."

But when he looked in
his bowl, it was empty.
The burglar had eaten
his porridge!

Then Winston saw his
chair. It was broken
into tiny pieces!

He looked again at the muddy footprints.

They went into the hallway and up the stairs . . .

Winston felt his heart thump.

The burglar was still here!

Winston's fur stood

on end.

Slowly, he tiptoed up the stairs. He peeped into the bedroom and followed the trail

past Mr. Brown's enormous brass bed. . .
past Mrs. Brown's middle-sized bed. . . .

Then he heard a noise. Somebody was snoring!

Winston's heart thumped harder.
Somebody was lying in his bed!
Winston couldn't look. He squeezed his eyes
shut and tried to make himself feel brave.

He thought of his stolen porridge and his broken chair. He puffed out his chest – and he GROWLED!

Winston heard a scream and he felt something brush past him. He opened his eyes, but the room was empty. The Somebody had gone!

Winston rushed to the window. There below him was the pigsty, and right in the middle of the pigsty, covered in mud, was the strangest creature Winston Brown had ever seen.

It struggled to its feet, looked up at Winston, and ran away through the forest.

Winston raced down the stairs.

Mr. and Mrs. Brown had just walked through the door.

"There was a burglar!" said Winston. "Look!"

Winston showed Mr. and Mrs. Brown the
footprints, and his empty bowl, and his
broken chair. He told them how he had
growled, and how the burglar had run away.
"What a brave little bear!"
they both said proudly.
"I'm NOT little!" said Winston,
looking up at Mr. Brown.

Mr. Brown reached down and swung Winston up, high into the air and onto his shoulders. It was the best feeling in the world.

Mr. Brown laughed. "There!" he said.
"You're a BIG bear now, Winston Brown!"

Activities to Enjoy

If you've enjoyed this story, you might like to try some of these simple, fun activities with your child.

Play the matching game

Continue the big-and-little theme by asking your child to make adult and baby picture cards. Make adult and baby cards for eight animals (16 cards in total). Then play a matching game. Mix up the cards and lay them face down. Take turns turning over two cards at a time. When a player turns over matching adult and baby cards, they keep them. The player with the most pairs wins!

Growing-up chart

Use a growing-up chart to praise your child for the grown-up things she does, and encourage her to do more things for herself. Ask your child what things she didn't used to be able to do, such as riding her bike. Then ask her to think of things that she can't do yet, perhaps tying her laces or making her bed. Make a chart with boxes to check beside the list of activities. Check the things your child can do now and check other things as she learns to do them.

Hide-and-seek

Play at being Winston and the "Somebody." The person playing the burglar hides, and the person playing Winston has to find the burglar. You could also play this game with toys. Pretend one of your child's toys is the "Somebody" and hide it. Then ask your child to be Winston and find the toy.

Making footprints

After it has been raining and the streets are beginning to dry, put on some waterproof shoes and go out to look for puddles. Make a trail of footprints like the ones left by the "Somebody" in the story. Or your child could print pictures with paint. Lay down lots of newspaper and have water and towels ready to clean up the mess!

Other Share-a-Story titles to collect:

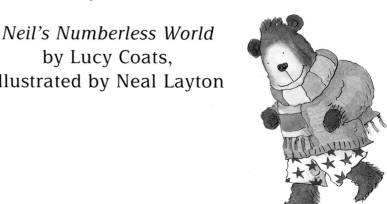